You Can't Rush A Cat

For Jessica
KB

For my mother, Joan Watts
LEW

National Library of Canada Cataloguing in Publication Data
Bradford, Karleen

You can't rush a cat / Karleen Bradford ; Leslie Elizabeth Watts, illustrator.

ISBN 1-55143-247-1

1. Cats--Juvenile fiction. I. Watts, Leslie Elizabeth, 1961- II. Title.

PS8553.R217Y68 2003 jC813'.54 C2003-910452-4

PZ7.B72285Yo 2003

First published in the United States, 2003

Library of Congress Control Number: 2003103724

Summary: Jessica shows her grandfather that it takes great thought and patience to win over the little wild cat that has moved into the basement.

Teachers' guide available from Orca Book Publishers.

Orca Book Publishers gratefully acknowledges the support of its publishing programs provided by the following agencies: the Department of Canadian Heritage, the Canada Council for the Arts, and the British Columbia Arts Council.

Design by Christine Toller
Printed and bound in Hong Kong

Orca Book Publishers
1030 North Park Street
Victoria, BC Canada
V8T 1C6

Orca Book Publishers
PO Box 468
Custer, WA   USA
98240-0468

05 04 03 • 5 4 3 2 1

You Can't Rush A Cat

KARLEEN BRADFORD & LESLIE ELIZABETH WATTS

ORCA BOOK PUBLISHERS

Jessica went to visit her grandfather.

He lived by himself and sometimes he got lonely.

When she got there, her grandfather was sitting on the back step holding a bowl of milk.

"There's a wild little cat in the bushes," he said. "She must be hungry, but she won't come out."

"You can't rush a cat, Granddaddy," Jessica said.

"I guess you're right," her grandfather answered.

He left the bowl of milk on the patio and they went inside.

When Jessica peeked out later on, the bowl was empty.

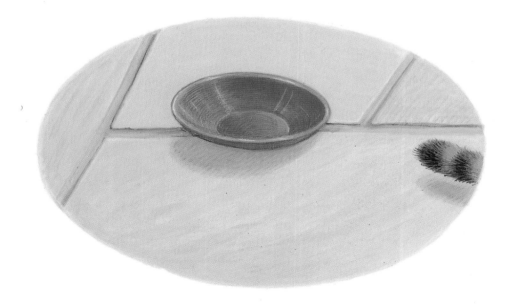

The next day was cold and rainy. After breakfast, Jessica's grandfather went to the back door and looked out. He called, "Here, kitty, kitty. Here, kitty, kitty."

Jessica thought she saw one of the bushes move, but it might have been the wind.

"That cat must be wet and miserable out there," Jessica's grandfather said. "Why won't she come in?"

"You can't rush a cat, Granddaddy," Jessica said.

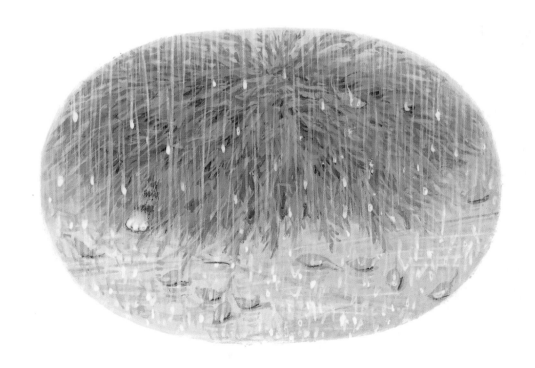

That night her grandfather left the kitchen window open just a bit. He called the cat again, but she did not appear.

The next morning, muddy paw prints crossed the kitchen windowsill. They led onto the counter, across the kitchen floor and down into the cellar. Jessica's grandfather grinned.

"Now we've got her," he said as he shut the window.

Jessica followed her grandfather down the cellar stairs.
"Come on out, cat," Grandfather called. "I've got fish!"
Jessica thought she heard a noise over by the furnace,
but it might have been the old house creaking.

"Why won't that silly cat come out?" Jessica's grandfather said.
"You can't rush a cat, Granddaddy," Jessica said.
They left the bowl of fish down there, along with some water,
and went back upstairs.

The rain turned to snow that week.

"That foolish cat must be freezing down there,"
Jessica's grandfather said.

It was cold in the cellar. Every day he put more food
and water out for the cat. He bought a litter box and put it
down there, too. The food disappeared and the litter box

got used, but of the wild little cat there was no sign at all.

"I'm beginning to think that's a ghost cat we've got in our cellar," Jessica's grandfather said. "I sure wish she'd come up where it's warm."

"You can't rush a cat, Granddaddy," Jessica said.

The next day, as they were finishing their breakfast at the kitchen table, a blur of orange flew up the cellar stairs, streaked across the kitchen and headed for the dining room. Grandfather was after it like a shot.

"She's under there," he whispered. He was on his knees on the dining room floor, peering under a big sideboard.

Jessica knelt beside him. Away back in the corner, two bright eyes glimmered at her.

"Now, kitty, come on out of there," Grandfather wheedled. "Please, kitty?"

The cat didn't budge, but Jessica thought she heard a faint purr.

That evening they sat by the fire and Grandfather read a story to Jessica. The wind was howling around the windows and the snow was turning into a blizzard. It was warm in the house, though, and cozy.

"At least that silly little cat isn't outside in all this," Grandfather said. "But I wonder when she's going to be sensible and come out to keep me company."

Jessica wondered, too. She was going home the next day. Was she never going to see that cat?

Early the next morning, before her grandfather was awake, Jessica tiptoed down the stairs from her bedroom. She had a plan.

First, she rinsed out the cat dishes that Grandfather had put in the corner of the kitchen and filled them with fresh food and water. Then she sat down and began to sing.

She started with "The Three Little Kittens Who Lost Their Mittens," went on to "Pussycat, Pussycat, Where Have You Been?" then "Ding Dong Bell, Pussy's in the Well."

She stopped singing that one, though. The cat might not like it, she thought. So she switched quickly to "The Owl and the Pussycat Went to Sea."

When Jessica finished singing all the cat songs she knew, she began to talk.

"If I were a cat," she said, "I would be getting pretty hungry for my breakfast right about now."

A slight scurrying noise came from the dining room.
Jessica held herself as still as she could.

"If I were a cat," she said, "I would love to have my ears rubbed right about now."

A small orange face peeked around the dining room door. Jessica pretended not to notice.

"If I were a cat," Jessica said to the ceiling, "I would love to curl up in somebody's lap right about now and see just how loud I could purr."

A soft, warm, furry little body brushed up against her hand. She moved one finger and started to scratch it, but she did not look down.

A small purr started up. It got louder and louder and louder, until, with a thump, the cat jumped right into her lap. Two tiny feet began to knead her leg. Jessica felt pinpricks as little claws dug in and out.

Finally, Jessica looked down, straight into the greenest eyes that she had ever seen.

When Jessica was ready to leave that afternoon, she ran into the living room to say one last good-bye to her grandfather. He was sitting by the fire in his favorite chair. Curled up in his lap was the little cat. Grandfather was reading a story to her and scratching her ears.

Jessica smiled.

"See, Granddaddy?" she said. "I told you. You just can't rush a cat!"